RAIDERS OF THE LOST ARCHIVES

BY MICHAEL DAHL
ILLUSTRATED BY PATRICIO CLAREY

STONE ARCH BOOKS
a capstone imprint

Secrets of the Library of Doom is published by
Stone Arch Books, an imprint of Capstone.
1710 Roe Crest Drive
North Mankato, Minnesota 56003
www.capstonepub.com

Library of Congress Cataloging-in-Publication Data is available on the Library of Congress website.

ISBN: 978-1-4965-9719-9 (library binding)
ISBN: 978-1-4965-9900-1 (paperback)
ISBN: 978-1-4965-9738-0 (ebook PDF)

Summary: Deep within the Library of Doom, raiders are searching for the treasure of the Lost Archives. When the thieves capture a young worker to guide them through the mazelike shelves, will the boy be forced to betray the Librarian?

Designed by Hilary Wacholz

Printed and bound in the USA.
PA117

TABLE OF CONTENTS

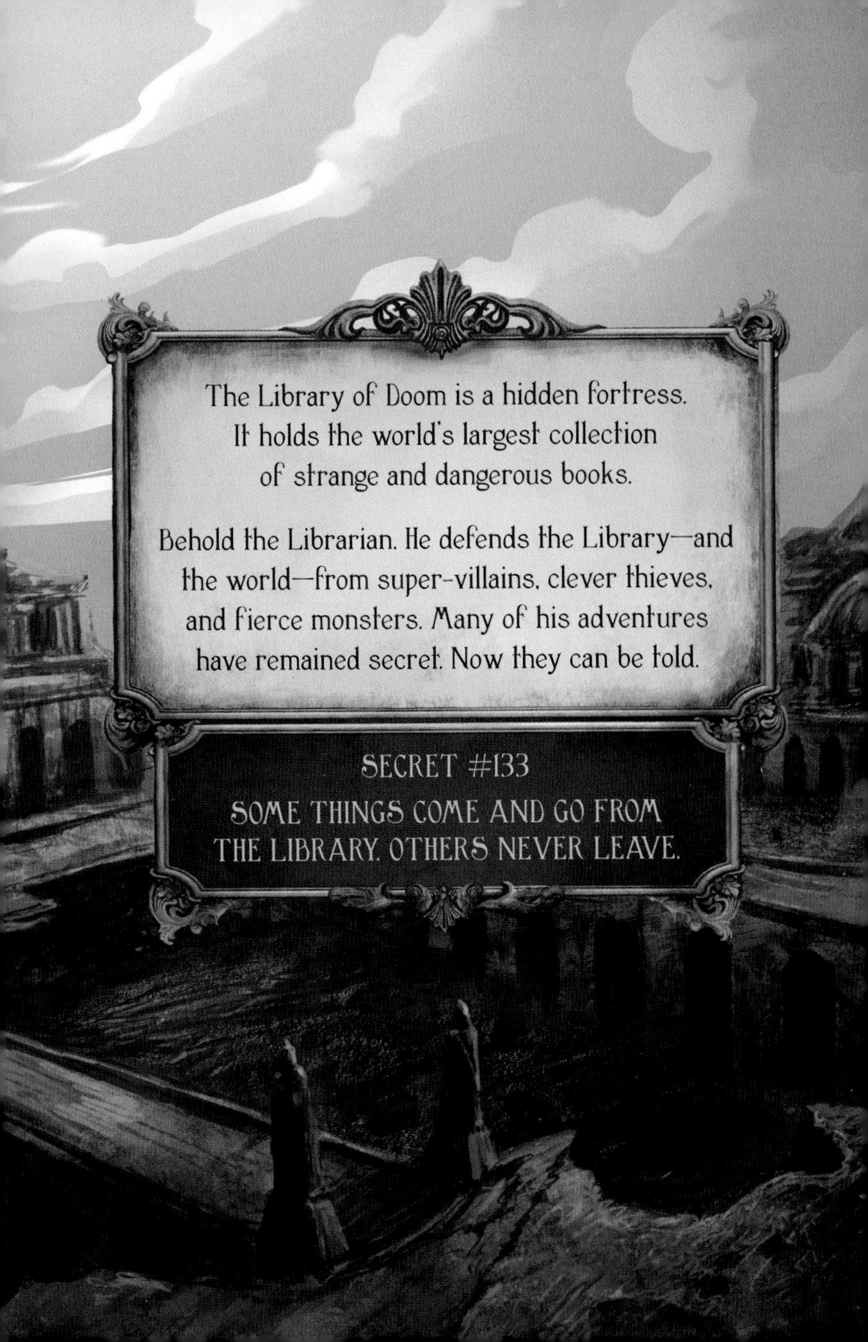
The Library of Doom is a hidden fortress.
It holds the world's largest collection
of strange and dangerous books.
Behold the Librarian. He defends the Library—and
the world—from super-villains, clever thieves,
and fierce monsters. Many of his adventures
have remained secret. Now they can be told.
SECRET #133
SOME THINGS COME AND GO FROM
THE LIBRARY. OTHERS NEVER LEAVE.

Chapter One

BELOW THE FOLD

A huge waterfall roars deep underground.

THHHOOOOOOOM!!!!

It falls from a hidden cliff called the Fold. The water is black, like INK.

Below the Fold, the waterfall ends in a deep pool. The pool **CHURNS** and bubbles.

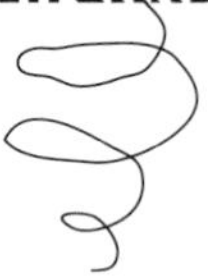

A stream flows from the pool. It flows into the darkness between two rocky walls.

Bookshelves are carved into each wall. Behind these walls are more walls, with more books.

The walls form a giant maze lit by BLUE FLAMES.

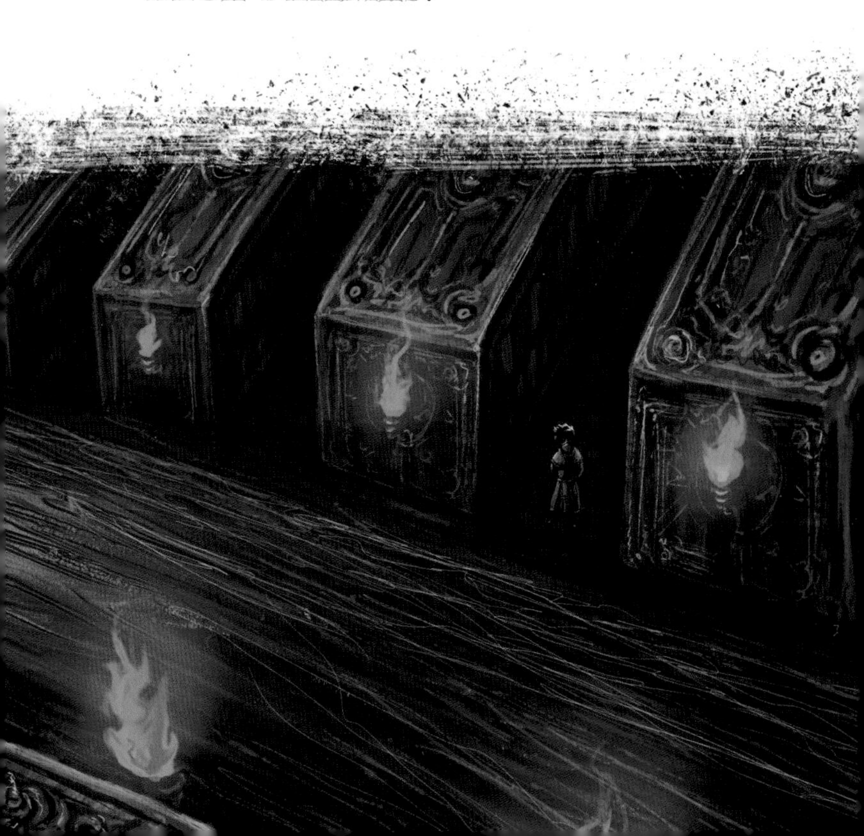

A young boy walks quietly between the walls. He wears a **LONG** blue robe.

A blue scarf is tied across his mouth.

He is a SILENT ONE.

The Silent Ones are a secret order of young readers.

Each of them has taken a vow of silence.

They work DEEP within the Library of Doom.

This boy is carrying a box full of papers.

He does not look at the stream flowing past the rocky walls.

He does not see the **SHADOW** rising from the black water.

Chapter Two

INK HORNS

A **SHARP** horn rises from the stream.

Below the horn is a helmet.

Below the helmet is a man with GLEAMING eyes.

More men **RISE** from the black water. They are raiders.

They carry long, **DEADLY** swords.

The raiders move to the edge of the INKY stream.

They climb out, but their boots make no sound.

¤ ¤ ¤

The silent boy walks through the MAZE of shelves without stopping.

There is no light except for the BLUE FLAMES hanging in the air.

There is no sound except for the **ROARING** waterfall.

The box of papers is heavy in the boy's hands.

After a while, he sees the empty shelf where the box belongs.

Then, metal gloves **REACH** out from behind him.

Chapter Three

THE RAIDERS

Two raiders hold the boy **TIGHTLY**.
Another raider grabs the box.

The boy has vowed to never speak, so he cannot yell. He cannot call for help.

"Where are the Lost Archives?" says the captain of the raiders.

Then the captain sees the blue scarf covering the boy's mouth.

"A Silent One!" **SHOUTS** one of the raiders.

"Impossible. They are only a legend!" says another.

The captain **PUSHES** the boy to the ground. "Since you will not speak," he says, "show us where the Archives treasure is hidden!"

The FRIGHTENED boy turns away from the men.

He uses his hand to make a letter in the **dark** air.

Chapter Four

"TAKE US . . . OR ELSE!"

The raider holding the box of papers yells. The box is SHAKING.

Suddenly, the papers **FLY** out. Hundreds of papers whirl around in a powerful wind.

FFFWWWSHHOOOOO!

The box falls to the ground. More papers fly into the air.

The papers rush together to **FORM** a giant ball.

The ball **SHRINKS** into a different shape.

A body.

Thunder rumbles.

The papers are gone. Instead, the LIBRARIAN floats above the raiders.

"I came as soon as I got your signal," the Librarian tells the boy. "Even a silent letter has **POWER**."

The Librarian looks at the captain. "Nothing leaves the Archives," he says.

The captain and his men surround the boy. They point their **LONG** swords at him.

"Take us to the Archives," the captain tells the Librarian. "**OR ELSE!**"

Chapter Five

THE TIGER AND THE MAZE

The Silent One is FROZEN with fear.

The Librarian looks at the boy. Then he looks at the FALLEN box.

"Very well. I will show you to the Archives," says the Librarian.

The boy's eyes **WIDEN** in surprise. He shakes his head no.

The box begins to **SHAKE** again. The raiders look at it, puzzled.

"What's the problem?" the Librarian asks them. "Cat got your tongue?"

The rest of the papers FLY out of the box. They make the shape of a huge, snarling tiger.

RRRROOOOOOOAARRRRR!

The captain and his men turn and run. But the PAPER TIGER follows them.

It **CHASES** them deeper and deeper into the maze.

Two giant doors **SWING OPEN** in front of the raiders.

A stone sign above the doors reads: *LOST ARCHIVES*.

The tiger chases the men through the doors.

LOST
ARCHIVES

Inside is another, larger MAZE.

The men disappear down the dark hallways.

"They got their wish," says the Librarian. "Now they will WANDER the Archives forever."

The boy watches the GIANT doors slam shut.

The Librarian is gone. There is no sound except for the WATERFALL.

The boy's box sits at his feet. All the papers are back in place once again.

GLOSSARY

archive (AR-kive)—a place where important papers and books are kept

captain (KAP-tuhn)—a military leader

churn (CHERN)—to move around quickly in a circle, as if being stirred

legend (LEH-jund)—an old story that may or may not be based on true events or real people

maze (MAYZ)—a confusing path made of many halls and dead ends that is difficult to find your way through

order (OHR-duhr)—a group of people working together for the same goal

raider (RAY-dur)—a person who suddenly attacks and steals things

signal (SIG-nuhl)—an action or sound that gives information and tells someone to do something

vow (VOW)—a very serious promise

wander (WON-der)—to walk around without knowing where you are going

TALK ABOUT IT

1. What was the special signal that brought the Librarian to the boy? How did the hero come into the maze of bookshelves? Describe in your own words how it happened.

2. What do you think was the most exciting part of the story? Be sure to use examples from the text and art to back up your answer.

WRITE ABOUT IT

1. What do you think has become of the raiders? Write another chapter that describes what happens to the captain and his men in the Lost Archives.

2. The Silent One was afraid when the raiders grabbed him, but he was also brave. He was able to get help. Write about a time when you asked for help, even though you were scared. How did it go? How did you feel afterward?

ABOUT THE AUTHOR

Michael Dahl is an award-winning author of more than 200 books for young people. He especially likes to write scary or weird fiction. His latest series are the sci-fi adventure Escape from Planet Alcatraz and School Bus of Horrors. As a child, Michael spent lots of time in libraries. "The creepier, the better," he says. These days, besides writing, he likes traveling and hunting for the one, true door that leads to the Library of Doom.

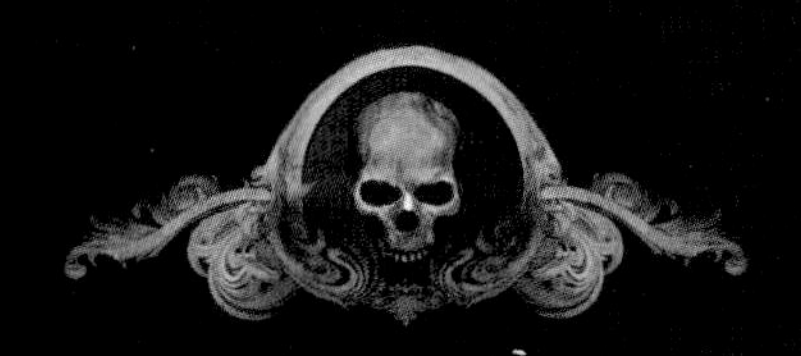

ABOUT THE ILLUSTRATOR

Patricio Clarey was born in 1978 in Argentina. He graduated in fine arts from the Martín A. Malharro School of Visual Arts, specializing in illustration and graphic design. Patricio currently lives in Barcelona, Spain, where he works as a freelance graphic designer and illustrator. He has created several comics and graphic novels, and his work has been featured in books and other publications.